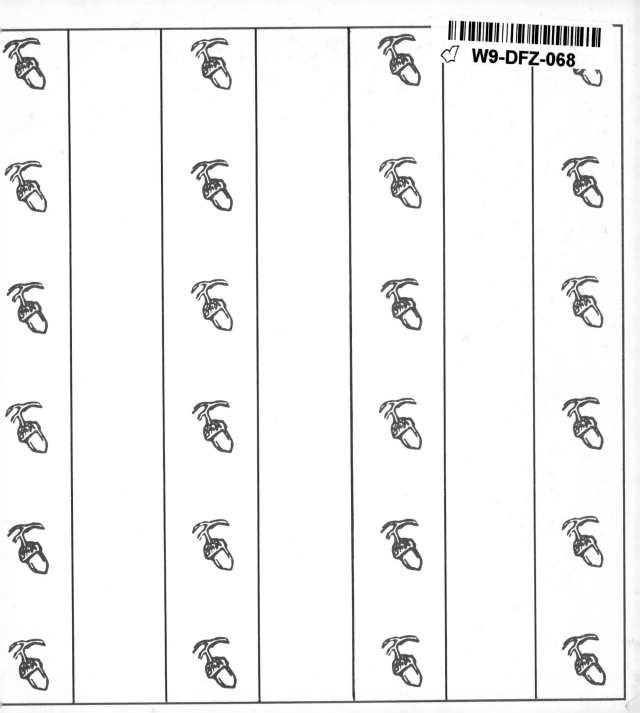

THE
BRATCHETS

THE BRATCHETS

by Edith Holden Cooke

illustrations by Lansing C. Holden

Holt · Rinehart · Winston *New York Chicago San Francisco*

Copyright 1936 by Oxford University Press

ISBN: 0-03-088444-6 (Tr)
ISBN: 0-03-088445-4 (HLE)
Library of Congress Catalog Card Number: 70-182779
Printed in the United States of America
Designed by Jane Byers Bierhorst

THE
BRATCHETS

This is the Bratchet family, Mr. and Mrs. Bratchet and the five little Bratchets.

They are saying: "How do you do? We are so glad to be in your book!"

You see how HAPPY they look.

Buster Bratchet was the biggest. Then Billy Bratchet.

Betsy and Bobsy Bratchet were next. They were twins.

Then came Benny Bratchet who was very small indeed but QUITE fat.

They LOOK like a very pleasant family.

But I am sorry to say they were NOT.
That is, not ALWAYS.

They sometimes fought over their midday
bones.

They were often very VERY naughty indeed.

Such BAD Bratchets!

It was hard on poor Mr. and Mrs. Bratchet.

Mr. Bratchet used to say: "I never was al-
lowed to behave like that in MY youth!"

And Mrs. Bratchet would say: "I'm sure
they do not take after me!"

"What SHALL we do?"

The worst of it was their house was very tiny. And there were so MANY children.

At the end of a rainy day Mother Bratchet was sure there must be DOZENS.

Though there were only five!

She and Father Bratchet used to go out in the rain for a little peace.

At last after a VERY bad day they were all
put to bed without any supper.

They knew they deserved it.

Buster Bratchet had broken a window with his baseball.

Though he did not MEAN to.

And Billy Bratchet had torn his BEST
clothes.

THAT was an accident, too.

Betsy and Bobsy Bratchet had spilled paint-water on their new bedroom rug.

WHY is paint-water always such a horrid color?

It made a LARGE spot.

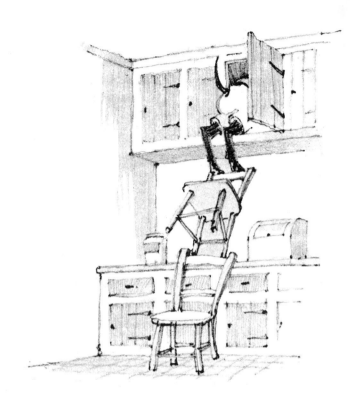

And Little Benny Bratchet had climbed up
to the pantry shelf and had eaten ALL Mother
Bratchet's strawberry jam!

He didn't WANT any supper after that!

But the others were HUNGRY.

They forgot how naughty they had been and felt very much abused.

Don't they look sad?

"Let's run away," said Buster Bratchet.
The others thought that was a fine idea.

All but little Benny Bratchet.

"What shall I do without my Mummy?" he
said.

But Betsy and Bobsy said: "We will be your
mothers."

Benny Bratchet thought that TWO might
be TOO many mothers.

But he said he'd try it.

So they all very softly rose from their beds
and climbed OUT of the window.

It was very dangerous and VERY exciting.

Then they all ran as fast as they could. When they stopped they found themselves in a big dark wood.

"My feet hurt," said Benny Bratchet.

"Oh Benny DEAR," said both his mothers.

But they helped him along.

There were lots of STUMPS.

And BRAMBLES!!

Then little Benny Bratchet began to cry.

The other Bratchets wondered what to do.

"We are his mothers," said Betsy and Bobsy.

"We must put him to bed."

"Where?" said Benny.

"We must find a hollow tree," said Buster.

So they found a hollow tree.

There were soft dry leaves in the hollow part of the tree that made nice comfy beds.

All five were asleep before you could say, "BRATCHET!"

And old owl stared at them and flew away. She lived in the tree.

Next morning they looked about them.

The tree was quite big, much bigger than their house at home.

"Let's live here always," said Buster Bratchet.

"I'm HUNGRY," said Benny Bratchet.

"Oh Benny DEAR,' said both his mothers.

But brave Billy Bratchet went out to explore.

In a few minutes he came back.

"I found a brook," he told them, "and lots of wild strawberries so we will have plenty to eat and drink."

Strawberries made Benny Bratchet think of his Mummy. He felt rather lonely and sorry about the jam.

This is the brook. A deer and her fawn are drinking there.

Billy saw them himself.

After their breakfast of berries, Betsy and Bobsy Bratchet went to work. They swept the inside of the Hollow Tree and washed it and brought in fresh leaves. Two beetles and three spiders decided to move to a new home.

Buster and Billy Bratchet stayed outside. They climbed almost to the top of the tree. It was hollow way up to a big branch.

"Let's make steps inside so we can have an upstairs," said Billy Bratchet.

At the end of the day the five Bratchets had made a fine house in the Hollow Tree.

Benny Bratchet WOULD get in the way.

The house looked like this outside.

It looked like this inside.

Every day they were busy working on their Hollow Tree House. They were MUCH too busy to be naughty.

They all would have been very happy if they had not missed Mother and Father Bratchet so much!

But they pretended they were VERY glad to be alone.

"We can stay up as late as we want to," said Buster Bratchet yawning.

"We can eat anything we like," said Billy Bratchet, pulling in his belt.

"I want my Mummy!" said Benny.

There wasn't much to eat, really except strawberries.

And they were SO tired of those!

And the twins wondered WHY they had
EVER wanted to be Benny's mothers.

Benny Bratchet wished they hadn't!

Little Benny Bratchet wanted to see his
Mummy and his Daddy more and MORE!
So one day he started home.
He walked and walked and WALKED!

At last he came to his old home.

And there at the door stood Father and
Mother Bratchet.

How GLAD his mother was to see him.

"But where are your dear brothers and sisters?" said Father Bratchet.

So Benny told them.

"A hollow tree? That sounds draughty!" said Mother Bratchet.

"It's very warm and comfy," said little Benny. "I wish you could see it."

So they decided to go back with him and look at it.

They took along a few things in case they
should stay.

When they reached the Hollow Tree the other little Bratchets were almost too happy for words.

Mr. and Mrs. Bratchet were very proud of their children's work.

And they thought the little Bratchets much improved.

All the neighbours came to call.

Mr. and Mrs. Bratchet decided to make the
Hollow Tree their home—after they had added a
few improvements.

BEST of all there was so much room that the five little Bratchets could make all the noise they wanted.

And Mother Bratchet cooked them all a HUGE big dinner.

There were all sorts of good things but NO strawberries!

And they were NEVER naughty any more!

At least as long as they were asleep.

And they all lived happily ever after!

This is the tail end of the Bratchets.

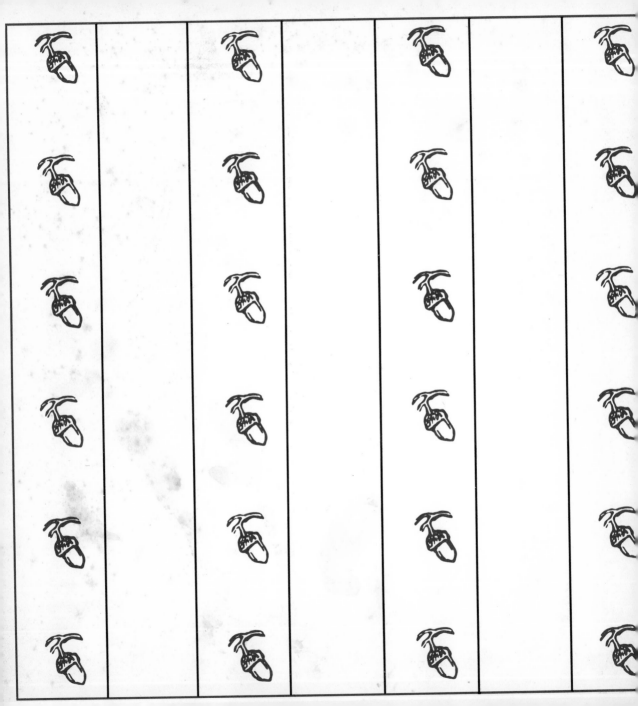